CALVIN MILLER

MR. FOUR FOOT THIRTEEN

The Story of Zacchaeus in Rhyme

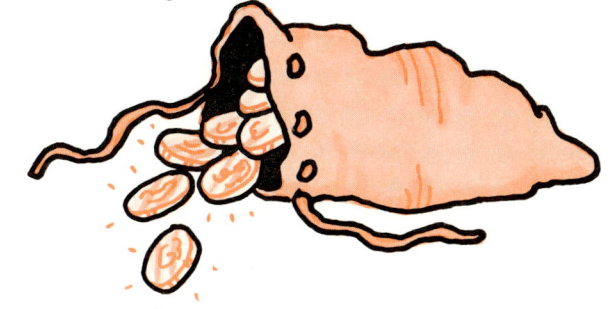

Illustrated by
Marc Harrison

THOMAS NELSON PUBLISHERS
Nashville

Copyright © 1987 by Calvin Miller
All rights reserved. Written permission must be secured from the publisher to use or reproduce any part of this book, except for brief quotations in critical reviews or articles.

Published in Nashville, Tennessee, by Thomas Nelson, Inc., and distributed in Canada by Lawson Falle, Ltd., Cambridge, Ontario.

ISBN 0-8407-6721-8   1 2 3 4—90 89 88

Zacchaeus, Director,
The Roman inspector,
Was Jericho Judah's
Unloved tax collector.

Zacchaeus was short.
Zacchaeus was lean.
Zacchaeus was barely
Four foot thirteen.
In a very tall crowd
He couldn't be seen.

Because Zacchaeus was short,
Some called him a wart.
Some called him a shrimp.
Some even called him
A wee-willy wimp!

But one name they called him
Made him turn green:
He despised being called
Mr. Four Foot Thirteen!

Zacchaeus loved only
One thing—that was gold!
He'd pile it in heaps
So when he grew old,
He still would have mountains
And mountains of gold.

For when he was timid,
Gold made him feel bold.
Gold made him feel warm
When the weather was cold.

Gold seemed like a friend
He could cling to and hold.
He was lonely and friendless,
For you may be sure
If you haven't a friend,
You're really quite poor.

Zacchaeus, Director,
Would knock on each door
In Jericho Judah
And shout, rant, and roar,
"Pay me your taxes!
So what if you're poor!
So what if your children
Are hungry or frail!
You must pay your taxes.
And if you should fail,
I'll chain you tonight
In the Jericho jail!"

Sometimes a mother
Would fall down and beg
And plead as she clutched
His short stubby legs.

"It would please us, Zacchaeus,
If you could just wait
Till the first of the month.
I promise I'll pay.
Just give me two weeks.
What else can I say?"

Zacchaeus just smiled
(As they begged and they wailed)
And ordered them chained
In the Jericho jail.

One day Zacchaeus
Woke up with a chill
And a very high fever.
He knew he was ill.

He stayed sick for weeks,
And he learned very well
That all of his gold
Could not make him well.

Day after day
Not one person came.
Zacchaeus was crying,
"I guess I'm to blame!
I've treated everyone
Evil and mean,
And now that I need them
They're not on the scene!"

On Tuesday he heard
A crowd out-of-doors.
Hundreds were shouting
Their joyous roars.

"Someone is coming
To old Jericho,
Someone so special
That each one should know."
Zacchaeus was sick,
But he too ran out
To see what this uproar
Was really about.

"Jesus is coming!"
The towering crowd
Was running around him
And shouting out loud.

Zaccheus was frantic.
"This crowd is so tall
I can't see a thing.
Oh, why was I born
Just four foot thirteen?"
He cried as he spied
A Sycamore tree.

He climbed up the tree
And called out to Jesus,

Then Jesus looked up!
"Zacchaeus, come down.
Come down for I say,
I'm coming, I'm coming
To your house today!"

Zacchaeus no longer
Felt sick and alone.
Zacchaeus and Jesus
Walked straight to his home.
They had a nice meal
And Zacchaeus allowed,
"Jesus, I'm glad
That I followed that crowd.

"And Jesus, because
You've been so kind to me,
I'm going to become
The best I can be.

"I'm through being heartless!
I'm through being mean!
Whatever I owe,
You'll see, I'll repay!
All that I stole or
Took wrongly away.

"I'll never again
Chain the poor, weak, and frail
For one single night
In the Jericho jail."

Zacchaeus, Director,
Became a new man.
He even seemed taller.
You know what I mean?
And no one believed
He was four foot thirteen.

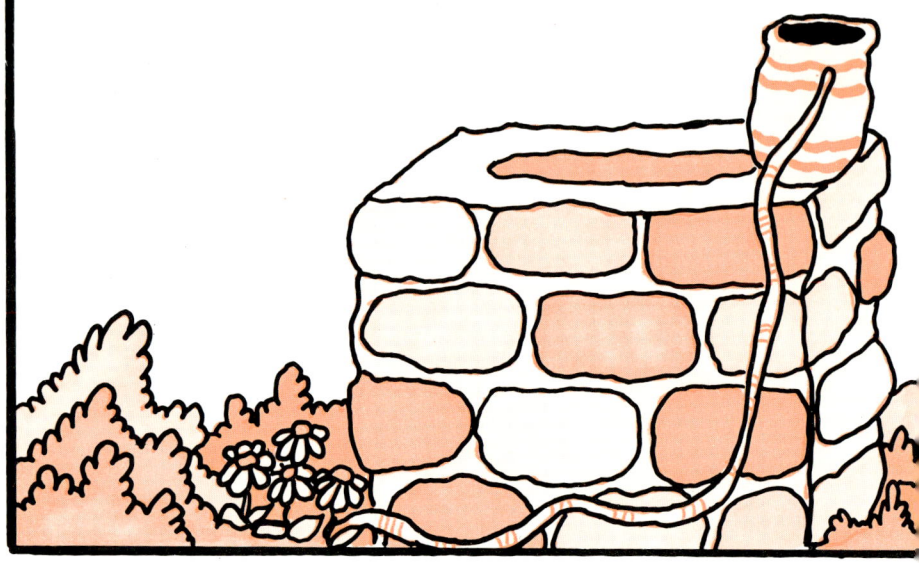

They loved him so much
And he had so much fun
That many now called him
Mr. Five Foot One!

You also can have
Just hundreds of friends.
Now is the perfect
Time to begin
To do unto others
Exactly as you
Would like everybody
To do unto you!